Hiding in the Shade

Hiding
In The
Shade

Discover Your Purpose.

Follow Your Dreams...

Kathryn Wiseman

ISBN-10: 0-9954403-1-X

ISBN-13: 978-0-9954403-1-9

www.fulfilled-life.com

Are you feeling a longing in your heart,

that you can't quite put into words?

A desire to be something,

but you're not quite sure what that is?

Are you feeling a quiet but persistent knocking,

that you can no longer ignore?

Your True Self, your Soul, may be calling you.

It may be time to fully express yourself in the world,

to be your most wonderful self,

to offer this gift to those around you

and to experience joy and exhilaration by

living your calling.

\- K.R. Jooste

Foreword

When we follow our hearts, life has some very exciting and fascinating surprises in store for us!

For me, one of those surprises is meeting up again with an amazing woman after many years, to find that we are kindred spirits. I met Kathryn more than twenty five years ago in South Africa, when she was friends with my sister. Kathryn always had a special glow about her, a beautiful smile that embraced you and blue eyes that welcomed you. As we grew up, we both followed our separate yet similar paths through medical school and then went to travel and live on different continents. Kathryn moved to Australia and I moved to the United States. We met from time to time in South Africa on family holidays and shared stories about our families. How incredible that we should connect again, all these years later, to find that we have had a similar journey. When I speak of our journeys, I don't mean the outward ones, that took us both to the far ends of the earth, from our birthplace in South Africa. I am speaking of the Inner Journey, the journey to the True Self, the calling to be who we are created to be, and to express this in the world with joy.

When Kathryn gave me her book, this gem which you now hold, I was so excited to read it. As I turned each page and read about Tawny, the young Eagle, who felt different from his lorikeet family, and experienced a restless boredom, I felt as if his experience was mine.

Are you feeling a longing in your heart, that you can't quite put into words? A desire to be something, but you're not quite sure what that is? Are you feeling a quiet but persistent knocking that you can no longer ignore? Your True Self, your Soul, may be calling you. It may be time to fully express yourself in the world, to be your most wonderful self, to offer this gift to those around you and to experience joy and exhilaration by living your calling.

In this story that Kathryn has written so beautifully, you may find the clear vision of what your calling is. Kathryn's words are truly inspired from that sacred space within her, where her Truth lives. She described to me, that as she wrote, she often felt that she herself was not writing at all, but that the words just flowed from her mind onto the page as if she were a medium for them, and the story unfolded as it should. I believe that this happens when we connect with that part of ourselves within, which is our Divine Self, the part connected to something greater than ourselves, to God. When we listen to that calling and dare to follow it, unimaginable things begin to manifest in our lives and we experience the joy of being our true selves.

If you feel this knocking today, some persistent voice

that tells you that there is something you are meant to be doing, then I encourage you to read Hiding in the Shade. Listen to your Soul calling you. You may recognize yourself as you read about Tawny and his own journey of self discovery. The simple beauty of Kathryn's metaphor for finding ourselves, and then expressing ourselves, is both poetic and pragmatic. It is poetic because the words are beautiful and the metaphor is so descriptive and apt. It is pragmatic because it seems to enable us to suddenly see ourselves with clarity. The narrative and fictional style seems to enable our mind to see the vision of our soul more clearly than many instructional books do.

You will find it exciting to read this, if you recognize yourself in it. It will shed light for you as to where you are on your own journey, and give you ideas as to how to proceed towards truly becoming all that you are meant to be, to expressing yourself authentically and joyfully in the world. This brings with it the incredible joy of contributing of yourself in a way that feels real and is so fulfilling. You will begin to feel engaged and fully alive.

Kathryn and I both wish you well on this spectacular inner journey. It may feel daunting – just take the first step by turning the page, and then continue the journey one step after another step. We wish you happiness, a deep connection to your true self, the courage to express yourself fully in this world, to forge your own path, and to flourish.

I am so grateful to Kathryn for this book. I was

surprised, delighted and honoured when she asked me to write this, yet she gave me far more than I could give her. Her book led me closer to the calling of my own soul, and I am so deeply grateful. Kathryn is truly standing in her own Light, her own Truth. She is bold and courageous. By standing in her light, she will encourage others to stand in theirs.

Kathryn's book will inspire you and give you the courage to follow your dreams and to listen to the voice of your soul. She has found her gift of wisdom, discernment and vision, and the world is blessed that she is expressing this and sharing it.

May you flourish and be happy!

Karen R Jooste, MD MPH,

Assistant Professor of Pediatrics, Duke Pediatrics Primary Care. Practice Course Faculty, Duke University School of Medicine.

Founder of Flourish: workshops and coaching, which facilitate vibrant wellness through writing and mindfulness.

Preface

Knowing the insightful person Kathryn is I looked forward to reading her book with great anticipation.

I was not disappointed.

Hiding in the shade unearths the very real longings and fears that so many of us struggle with most of our lives.

Through her questions at the end of each chapter, Kathryn invites us to probe a little deeper into the psyche of our souls, to really listen to our own hearts and dare to follow our dreams.

In her beautiful style Kathryn has tapped into the deeper parts of all of us and showed us the way out of the dark tunnels of fear and of misunderstanding our true selves.

This is a must read for anyone wishing to unearth their dreams and find the courage and exhilaration of doing that for which we were born.

Hiding in the shade leads us on a journey to discover

and answer life's biggest questions, "Who am I?" and "What was I born for?"

In this beautiful story Kathryn has skillfully used her life coaching skills and knowledge to shine the light on some foundational life questions. We can discover more about ourselves by asking the right questions which brings life transforming awareness. This is important for everyone to read.

Kathryn also shares her own experience on this journey with beautiful vulnerability

Read it and you will be challenged but not disappointed!

Peter and Karen Nicholes

Southern lights Church, Network leaders. Changing hearts, changing nations.

Acknowledgements

I would like to first and foremost thank my husband Greg. You have an incredible love for me and an endless patience with me. Thank You! During the many years I spent desiring something, yet not feeling sure what that something was, you tirelessly encouraged me in each new endeavor. You have somehow always seen great potential in my ability to achieve whatever I set out to do. You have patiently endured my tears of many frustrated endeavors and have helped me to turn these tears into laughter, to not take myself so seriously and to find the fun in each experience we've journeyed through.

I have journeyed alongside you, watching you live out your life's true calling with clear vision and purpose. This has given me such hope and inspiration, because I have witnessed firsthand the joy and fulfillment you have in gifting those around you by living your calling. You have helped me to see what is possible for all of us. Thank you for the role model our sons have in you.

I would like to also thank my sons, Cullam and Matthew. Wow. Where do I begin? Each day I thank God for the abundant joy of being your mom. You have both grown into exceptional young men who have so much to offer to the world around you. You each have remarkably different personalities and being a part of each of your unique journeys has taught me invaluable lessons about discovering and being true to yourself. I know this book will bless you both as you each journey along your own path.

To all the coaches I have met through Frazerholmes Coaching, Jaemin, Mark, Sue. Thank you! Your teaching has changed my world. I finally understood why I kept going around in circles, doing the things that were 'working perfectly' for me but all the while sabotaging my growth and keeping me small. Your training has given me wings to fly. Without you all, this book would not exist.

To Teegan Nash from Verve Design studio who designed my cover art and so much more. You have helped me develop a brand that is unique and true to me. You have helped me to see more clearly what I have in front of me. Your continued advice and wisdom and knowledge are greatly appreciated!

To Emily Heill for the tireless hours involved with editing this book. I have not met you in person, yet loved working with you online. You are a gentle soul. Professional, accurate and amazingly time efficient! Thank you for journeying beside me during this season. I will definitely be calling on you again in the future!

To Julie Rice, my coach during the season of writing this book. I am often in awe of the people God brings along our path in perfect time and place. I feel so blessed to have met you. This journey has proved to me that having a Life Coach to shine new perspective, bring clarity and wisdom to where you are at in this moment is invaluable. Thank you for your effective coaching skills over the past weeks. You have given me the courage to persevere and publish this book. Thank you!

To God, who through your Holy Spirit living in me whispered this story for me to share with the world. You are love, joy, peace, patience, kindness, goodness, faithfulness, gentleness and self-control. You are the light to my path. You are the air I breathe. I live this life for you.

Table of Contents

Prologue

Have you ever been through a season of feeling restless or bored? I am not talking about a single afternoon of boredom…or even a few days. I am talking about a season… a more long-term restless boredom. You would really like for something to change, but you just can't seem to put your finger on it. "I wonder if there is something that I could do differently?" you ask. Yet, at the same time, in that same season, you also feel reasonably content. The restlessness is mild and you tell yourself that it's nothing, and that "this too shall pass." After all, everything around you seems okay. Everyone else seems happy enough with the status quo. So you settle into a mediocre kind of existence. A comfortable sense of rhythm evolves. You carry on carrying on. And you notice that in spite of the mediocrity, you become convinced that you are adequately satisfied with life as it is.

Then one day you hear a talk by someone who inspires you, or you read something that stirs your heart and you start to wonder… "Hmm, could there be more to life than this?" "Could there be an adventure out there with my own name on it?" Excitement creeps in and you start to wonder. Your wondering turns to dreaming and before you know it, your dreams feel like a possible reality. "Could this dream be more than just a dream?" you ask. Yet the more you ponder your dream, the more you start to think of all the things you will need to research and do, or to change and to invest in. The reality of what it could mean to follow through with your heart's desire sinks in. It all feels too big. It feels like there is too much at stake. So you decide that it's all just silly. It's all just a dream anyway. You decide that it is probably better to just stay where you are, in the comfort of what you know. You convince yourself that it's not that bad feeling a little bit bored after all!

Chapter One.

Let me introduce you to Tawny. He is a beautiful, fun-loving young eagle who lives in one of the giant lush mango trees near the banks of the brown river. He is the only one of his kind that lives in this great big mango tree. Yet, he is never lonely or alone because he is surrounded by a large happy family of sorts. This family is made up of quite a lively variety of creatures. Allow me a minute to introduce you to a few of them. Lulu is a bright and feisty rainbow lorikeet. She is one of many as she has a fairly large number of brothers and sisters—not to mention all of her cousins. The lorikeets are as lively as they are colourful and when they really get excited, the noise they make drowns out everyone and everything else within a mile of their great big mango tree. Then there is the grand pigeon family that thankfully keeps some semblance of order among the tree's residents. Mr Pigeon has a real authoritative aura about him and feels he has achieved well during his day when all is in order around and within their tree as the sun begins to go down. Let us not forget Phillip, the possum, and Petra his sister. They mostly keep huddled up together in a deep burrowing hole just above the third huge old gnarled branch up from the ground. They love to come out at night and after a scuffle through the leaves and a good lot of munching, they bound out for an evening of adventure before returning to their hole a few hours later. There are many smaller creatures of other kinds too that add to the hustle and bustle of life in the great big mango tree. These include spiders, small lizards and tiny tree frogs to name a few. These little creatures tend to come and go and in Tawny's mind, they would not be considered relatives exactly. He would more likely call them 'dinner'. Tawny spent most of his days flying about with Lulu and her siblings, and, at dusk, would have a lively chat to the possum pair about their previous evening's adventures. The one important fact I have not yet shared with you about Tawny is that at this time in my story, he hasn't yet discovered that he is an eagle.

Now, if you were to have had a conversation with Tawny a few weeks ago, and were to ask him how his life was going, he would tell you that he was comfortable, happy and at peace living in the shade of the giant mango tree. He would tell you how he loved to hang out with Lulu and her family. They would dart and dive from branch to branch and disappear through tiny spaces. He would try his best to keep up with them, but was often too big to really play as wildly as he longed to. He would make up for this by secretly pretending that he was a king, and that the giant mango tree was his magnificent castle. The shade of this magnificent tree was his delight and his court. This had to be kept a secret of course, because the others would laugh at him if they knew how silly his thoughts were.

He would also tell you how he loved to feast on lizards, ants and spiders and, when really lucky, he'd even catch a small rabbit! Now that was a feast to celebrate! The others in his family seemed to be happy enough to settle for a meal of pollen, nectar and fruit. Tawny could not fathom how this diet could satisfy! He did, however, love the mango season!!! He really LOVED eating mangos! Just thinking about tearing away at their skin to get to that sweet sticky yellow-orange juice and pulp was enough to make him puff out his chest and fluff out his feathers! He could almost conjure up the smell of their sweet scent in his mind. In short, he was adequately satisfied with life as he knew it in the shade of the huge mango tree. Its great branches and its busy inhabitants were a comfort to him. However, he would then pause to ponder that maybe, just maybe he was a little bit different to the rest of his family and maybe, just maybe, something significant was missing.

Your turn

Where is that place that you would call your comfy place in the shade?
When are you most comfortable right now?
Who lives with you in your shade?
Are you one of a kind? Or do you blend in well with those around you?
What do you feast on? What do you feel you miss out on?
What do you dream about?
Do you feel a slight nudging that maybe something significant could be missing?

____

____

____

____

____

____

____

____

____

____

____

____

____

____

Chapter Two

Then one fine morning, after yet another mango season had come and gone, while perching right on the very top of the lush giant mango tree, a teeny tiny speck of a thought, like a vague light whisper floated lightly down, down, down and landed gently on top of Tawny's head. He was almost not quick enough to catch it, or astute enough to recognise it. Yet on this day, the light touch luckily tickled him enough to interrupt his usual thoughts, and he allowed it to settle and then to sink a bit deeper into his mind. This new thought went something like this: "What if I were to fly so high up, up, up into the sky that I could see out further and wider that I've ever seen before? What if I could then fly out as far as I could see? Oh!!!! What an adventure that would be!!!" These new thoughts sent delicious ruffles through his feathers. He was so excited that he decided to go and share them with Lulu and her siblings. He listened for their chirpy noises and flew off to find them. Just before he had a chance to blurt out his new thoughts, he remembered how often they had laughed at his ideas in the past and told him how silly he was. This got him wondering "….is this new thought also just silly?" Maybe. So instead, he decided to keep this thought safe inside his own mind for the time being. Just then Lulu darted in and landed on a branch above his head, calling him to join her and the other lorikeets. So for the time being, he shelved his secret new thought and took off to play with the others.

As he took off to play, another thought caught his attention. It was as though for the first time he realised that trying to keep up with these feisty little lorikeets and their silly games was not really great fun after all. The more he thought about this, the more he realised that this is how he had felt for quite a long while already. But what else was there to do? Surely hanging out with his friends was better than sitting on his own all day.

So that afternoon as they darted here and there, in and out, Tawny decided to watch closely for any clues he might have previously missed. Maybe he would notice one of the others feeling the same way he did. As he watched them, he noticed again how brightly beautiful their colourful feathers were. He noticed how they loved sucking on nectar and pollen, how they loved chirping noisily to each other. He noticed how because they were so much smaller than he was, they could have enviable fun darting through small gaps between branches, and playing hide and seek so smartly. Suddenly, Tawny felt lonely. He felt like he was the only one who was different. He felt big and clumsy compared to the others. He also knew he was not nearly as pretty with his dreary mottled brown feathers. And he realised that he was without doubt the only one who looked bored.

All this thinking made him feel even more sad and gloomy. Was this it? Would life always be like this? He wished he could wake up one morning with the same colourful feathers that Lulu had, and with the same zest for life that they all seemed to have. So before anyone else could notice his sadness, Tawny flew off on his own. He flew up and up and up. Before long, he realised that he had flown about as high as he had ever dared before and instantly felt his sadness drift away. He swooped and twirled and let out his own unusual call. He soon felt happy again and so flew back to the comfort of the shade of the familiar giant mango tree.

Once settled back on his favourite branch, he felt peaceful again. "Everything is good" he told himself. "Each time I feel a bit bored, I'll just fly up high and play on my own, the way I like most and that will make things right." Just as he was keeping his eyes open for some tasty morsel, Mr Pigeon hopped over to his side. "Tawny, young fellow" he chirped, "I noticed you fly up so very high today. I would rather you didn't fly so high. What if you get lost up there, or cannot get back to us? What if something bad happened to you while you were so far away up there? Please, Tawny, no more!" he chirped sternly. Tawny sat very still. He was flabbergasted. "Oh, okay" he mumbled.

He felt like the wind had just been knocked out of him. But I just have to fly up high for my own happiness… I just have to his thoughts screamed inside his head. He resolved then and there that next time, he would just have to plan to sneak away when no one was looking. Yet deep down, he liked Mr Pigeon and didn't want to upset him, so he knew he would do as he was told.

That night as he slept, he dreamt again about the tiny thought that had visited him for the first time only a few hours earlier. He dreamt he was flying higher than he ever thought possible, looking out wider and further than he could ever have imagined before. This dream visited him each night for the next few nights, and the thoughts about his dream lingered every day over the next few days. He was so glad that he had not mentioned the dream to anyone else so that no one could tell him to stop dreaming it. Just knowing that he could visit this dream any time he chose kept him happier than he had been in a long while. Then one day he noticed that he had become so familiar with this new dream that it no longer felt new. It almost felt like it had been there for as long as he could remember. And so he began to play with it more and more. He started to toss it into the air. Up and down, up and down it went. He played with it day in and day out for a few weeks. And without even realising it, the thought grew into a dream that overflowed from his mind and settled deep inside his heart. Still, he spoke of this to no one because, after all, it was just a silly old dream…Was it not?

Your turn

What dreams do you have that you have not yet brought
to the front of your mind?
What dreams do you have that rest lightly on your mind,
or knock loudly on your door?
What dreams do you have that leave you feeling excited
and exhilarated?
Do your dreams seem impossible? Do your dreams feel
so so far away and way too big to ever consider? What
dreams do you have that you push away only for them to
come rolling back?
What dreams do you suppress because you think that
that is all they are… silly dreams?
Do you push your dreams down to keep others happy or
because others tell you that they are not possible?

____

____

____

____

____

____

____

____

Hiding In The Shade

13

Chapter Three

There Is Great Comfort in the Shade...Until It Gets Too Cold

Some days, Tawny would throw his not-so-new and by now well-formed dream up really high, so that it would take a long while to come back down again. In those few seconds, waiting to catch it, he would let it wonder further and grow even larger. What would it really be like to be the adventurous explorer he dared to dream about? Just imagine how different it would be to sleep overnight up high in the branches of a huge unfamiliar tree, in an unknown savannah land! What if he found a place where rabbits were plentiful and trees bared mangos all year round? These thoughts would send a ruffle through his feathers. Some days, they would make him so excited that there were a few moments when he would lose himself entirely in his dream and almost really fly up and up and up…Then in a split second, he would jolt back to reality and shake himself free from the silliness and the fear, and fly back down to his comfy home in the shade of the giant mango tree. There, he would come face to face with the stern glare from Mr Pigeon who would always be watching and shaking his head.

Tawny started to feel trapped and frustrated. He had to find a way out! That's when he recognized that another incomprehensible thought had settled in his mind. "What would it really be like to leave the delicious cool shade of this mango tree that he knew so well and loved so much?" This thought felt absolutely crazy. It felt light and free, yet heavy and sad at the same time. It felt like a sudden whirlwind of turmoil in his mind. It was all too much. All too overwhelming. He shook himself to try to still his mind. And that's when he noticed it again, that now all too familiar sadness had come creeping back in. "What is happening to me?" he whispered. "I used to be happy. Life used to be fun…" and in that moment, a sad truth settled upon him. He was not only restless and bored. He felt stuck. Helpless and hopeless. He had no idea how to make things right again. He started to notice other things too. Lulu's jokes were no longer funny at all, and the little brown lizard that darted up the tree trunk was no longer such an exciting dinner option. "What is happening to me?" Tawny asked himself again and again. Feeling frustrated, he tried to enjoy the company of the others. He tried to make himself laugh and chat. He tried hard to just forget his silly dream. But it kept coming back, knocking, knocking, knocking.

"What if this dream isn't so silly after all?" "What if I did go?" "Could I just go?" "Would the others miss me?" "Would it be so bad to leave this tree?" The more he thought about it all, the more questions came rolling in. What about all the unknowns, the dangers, the what-ifs? "What if I get lost and can't ever make my way back to my castle in this giant mango tree? What if I never get to see my family again?" "What if going away ends up being even worse than where I am here? After all, this is my home." So Tawny kept bouncing these questions backwards and forwards, and eventually came to a final conclusion. As much as these dreams of exploring and adventuring exhilarated and excited him, there was just too much at stake. There was just too much to lose! What would he do without Lulu, and Phil, and these mangos, the familiarity, the safety, the comfort? And days passed. And weeks passed. And frustration and sadness and hopelessness grew, and finally Tawny lost all his joy.

Your turn

Does your dream keep bugging you?
Has your big vision grown clearer and larger? Do you find
yourself noticing it in more detail?
Does your dream feel like it is almost in arms reach?
Where could it take you? Can you see it? Can you feel it? What
do you hear? What do you smell? Taste? Does the place you are
at at the moment leave you feeling more and more frustrated or
irritable?
Uninspired or bored?
Have you noticed this nagging feeling of emptiness? Do you get
the feeling that something is missing?
Or else you may be asking: Is this all there is to this life?
Do you feel like you have lost your joy?
Do you feel like the risk is too big, the change is too scary and
you have too much to lose?

____

____

____

____

____

____

____

____

____

Chapter Four

Shining Light Enhances the Shade

T hen one slightly cloudy but bright night, months after the tiny spec had first floated down and gently kissed Tawny on the cheek, he heard an all too familiar sound from long ago. The deep, soft hoot-hoot he knew could only belong to one great friend that he loved. He could scarcely believe his luck! Suddenly, he felt like smiling again for the first time in a long long while. It felt like a flicker of unfamiliar hope had just licked his cheek. You see, that tiny speck of a dream had over time become so heavy that it felt like his heart would never ever feel joy again. Tawny had just earlier that same day finally resolved that the only thing he could think of doing to help himself was going to be to let it all out. He had decided he was going to finally tell someone all about his silly dreams. So what an amazing coincidence that this was the very same day that William, the wise old owl, had chosen to make his appearance. William had used to visit the tree frequently, but for some reason over the past few years, his visits had become more and more sparse. Yet here he was, on this bright night. Tawny could hardly believe his luck! This wise old owl was just the one to help him.

So he fluttered down towards where William had landed. "Hello William! How wonderful to see you" he cried. But before he could say much else, the colourful lorikeet family and the pigeon family had flocked over to join them. They all sat perched around the wise old owl enjoying listening to the stories he had brought to share about his travels. After a few hours, Tawny felt a long forgotten peace slowly trickle through him as he listened intently to everything that was going on. The other family members fought for their turn to speak, but Mr Pigeon took his usual stand of authority and spoke first…and longest.

Lulu and her siblings managed to get a chirp in here and there, but for the most, Tawny just sat quietly and listened to every word the wise old owl spoke. He was listening for any clues or hints that maybe his dream was not so crazy after all. Meanwhile, it did not pass the wise old owl's patient attention that Tawny was so unusually quiet and looked so unusually sad. Once everyone else had settled for the night, and Phil and Petra had scuffled off on their evening's mission, William swooped his way over to Tawny for the chat that he knew was the specific reason for his visit on this bright warm night.

You see, the wise old owl had over the years become intimately familiar with the voice of his great creator. The voice of God. He knew that God was the giver of dreams and joy and, most of all, the giver of life. William had discovered over the years that once you heard Gods voice giving you your dream, your call, your purpose, the best thing to do was to pay close attention and to follow it. William had discovered for himself that God certainly was the giver of a most fulfilled life, so long as you had the courage to follow Him. He had seen this pattern over and over in the life of so many creatures throughout his travels. You see, William had watched many creatures bravely answer their call. He had watched them soar to amazing heights, far greater than they ever would have believed their dreams could take them. He had experienced their joy, their adventure and the amazing fulfilment, happiness and peace that it brought them.

He had also sadly watched many others turn away from their dreams. He had watched them choose the safety of their known comfort and their familiar boundaries over the call of their "silly" and "crazy" dreams. He had also watched other creatures as they started to follow their dreams, but then decided they were too big, or too difficult or too challenging, and so had given them away. He had observed over and over that for these creatures, a certain shine would start to fade, and over time their joy would often be replaced with a dull boredom or a muddled confusion about what they were supposed to be doing. They would go about their days groaning and muttering "Is this all that there is to this life? Surely there is supposed to be more?" It is as though the comfort of their shade had actually now become too cold.

Your turn

Do you sometimes wonder if this is all that there is to this life?
Do you feel muddled and unclear about what you are created or
designed to be doing?
Do you sometimes feel as though you would rather be somewhere
else instead of where you are now?
What if you do follow your dreams?
What if you don't?

____

____

____

____

____

____

____

____

____

____

____

____

____

____

25

Chapter Five

It Is Okay to Step out from the Shade

So as William settled down next to Tawny on one of the higher gnarled branches of the great big mango tree he asked, "How are you doing, young friend?"Tawny answered "William! You have no idea how perfect the timing of your visit is. I am desperately needing to tell you all that has been going on in my heart and mind for so long now!"William smiled warmly and encouraged Tawny to let it all out. Tawny spent the next whole hour telling William in the finest detail all that he had been seeing and dreaming. He spoke with fervour and excitement and felt more alive than he had in ages being able to share his dream with William. However, as he came to the end of his story, his excitement faded as quickly as it had arrived and he let out a great big sad sigh. He nervously lifted his gaze to look into Williams face and what he saw truly astonished him. Rather than an expected knowing look that says "Now, Tawny, that was a silly story!", instead William's eyes were sparkling and he was grinning from ear to ear!

"Welcome to your life's mission, young Tawny!" hooted William. "I am delighted by the dream you have just shared with me! I have been waiting for days and days for you to be ready to speak about the things you have kept hidden in your heart for so long. This is absolutely marvellous!"

Tawny couldn't believe what he was hearing! He was stumped. Gobsmacked. His eyes were wide and his heart was pounding so loudly he felt sure it would wake up all the other animals in the tree. What!? William, the wise old owl, had known about his dreams all along!? How could this be? So he gave out a whispered but high pitched blurt "William! How could you have known I was having these dreams before you even arrived here?" William fluffed out his feathers and wound his head around to settle in for this most fabulous and enjoyable conversation. "Well, no, Tawny, it's not exactly what you are thinking. You see, a long time ago, I was once in the same place you are now regarding your dreams and thoughts. I was almost certain that I recognised a glimmer of this in you during my last visit. It is as though I can see it in others, because I was once there myself. I knew I needed to give you some time and then to return later to find out if what I had seen was correct.

You see, Tawny, these dreams come to all of us at some stage. The dream has always been there, even before you were born! Unfortunately for many, they shrug their dreams off or blow them away. I really did hope that you would hang on to yours and let it grow, and you have! Well done, young Tawny!" Tawny was quiet for a while. He still could hardly believe what he was hearing! "What did William mean when he spoke about being in the same place I am in now?" So he asked, "William, tell me about the time when you were where I am now. Did you have the same dream that I have had?" "No Tawny," replied William. "We all have different dreams, yet many of us ignore them or try our best to push them away. It is when we first allow ourselves to take notice of our big dreams that for a season, if we choose to hang on to the dream, we go through a process that becomes similar for all of us. And this is where I notice you are at now. The process always requires patience, discernment, wisdom, and a whole lot of courage. Often, just like you and like me, we require some wise counsel to understand what is required next."

"We are usually confronted with many questions which can leave us feeling overwhelmed and confused. We ask: Where did this dream come from? Is it for real? Am I supposed to hang on to it and follow it? Is it just silly? Is it even possible? What if following this dream means giving up a whole lot of what I know and am comfortable with? For some creatures, it is all these unanswered questions that cause them to let the dream go. From their perspective, life seems far less complicated without the dream, even though they know something is missing." Tawny felt like William had just been inside his head reading his exact thoughts. All those questions were the exact ones that he had been grappling with.

Your turn

How would you feel if someone affirmed that your deepest desires really are your life's mission?
Have you allowed yourself to take notice of your heart's desires?
Does your dream excite you enough to wake you and inspire you?
Does your dream burden you to make some changes?
How does it feel when you realise that some things will need to change if you were to ever consider following your dreams?
How do you feel about leaving your comfort zone to follow your dreams?
Would you need to walk away from where you are now to step into your dream?

____

____

____

____

____

____

____

____

____

____

____

____

Chapter Six

William noticed the perplexed look on Tawny's face and knew the time had come to share his own story with this younger fellow. "Let me tell you my story. It may help you to understand yours. Mine began a long time ago."

I was a very young owl, who enjoyed mucking around on most days… actually, my life until then had been much like yours. I had my friends and also my sister, so I always had company. I just assumed I was happy and content. We played all day and did the few chores we knew to do. Life was really rather uneventful back then, but I felt happy enough. Then one day, a great uncle of ours swooped in for a visit and to say hello to my parents. I had never seen him before this day, but had heard my parents speak about him often. I knew that my parents held him in high esteem. From the moment great Uncle Owl arrived until the moment he left, I couldn't keep my eyes off him. I found myself hanging on to absolutely every word he said.

He was so profoundly wise and yet also so incredibly down to earth, so strong and yet so gentle, so old and yet so young at heart. The things he shared about being happy and feeling fulfilled in living each day with purpose sounded so simple, so obvious and so true. I couldn't believe I had never heard this stuff before, yet at the same time I felt that somewhere inside me I had known these things all along. He shared the most amazing stories about all his travels. His stories were so astonishing and adventurous that I soon began to realise that my life as it was until then was way too mediocre and was definitely missing something.

Then one day, great Uncle Owl announced that he would be on his way again. After he had gone, I felt like I was left with a vacuum inside of me. I felt almost empty. This caused me to start my search. I was looking for something that would fill me up. Something to satisfy me. I started dreaming. About a week had passed when one night I had such a clear and vivid dream that when I woke up, I was confused for a moment about whether it was only a dream or actually real.

I had dreamt that great Uncle Owl was out searching for a wise young owl to mentor and to teach, someone who would carry over and continue the work he was doing because soon he would be too old. It was as though he was searching for a student to pass all his wisdom down to. Tawny, I just knew, with every fibre in me, that this was what I longed for more than anything! I had searched out my heart and had found my dream, my calling. I felt like I had stumbled upon a treasure chest that had my name on it.

I wanted to learn to be wise and discerning just like my great uncle. I wanted to go on adventures and missions just like he had done. For a moment, I became so excited, but my excitement was short lived because reality quickly began to sink in as I believed I was too small and would never be wise enough. How could I possibly ever have discernment like my great uncle? So, I guessed it was just a farfetched dream after all. Yet I held tight to my dream and as the weeks went by, like you, I played with it over and over, and so my dream continued to grow. I felt I couldn't share this with anyone because, of course, they would laugh at me. I would just casually, in a "oh-by-the-way" kind of way, ask my sister what she had thought about our great uncle, and his life story. It was as though she had not noticed him at all!!! I couldn't believe that she could be so disinterested. She was far more focussed on our cousin who had just given birth to the fluffiest little owlet you have ever seen. I now understand that this was because her big dream was just completely different to mine.

I, nevertheless, decided to hang onto my dream. In my dream, I was truly wise. I somehow had wisdom way beyond myself. I had wisdom and discernment for other creatures too and I saw myself flying all over the place, taking bits of wisdom to all kinds of creatures in all kinds of places and situations. I would ponder these things for ages, and then suddenly it was as though a switch inside me would flip, and I would catch myself thinking "Of course, this is totally silly and obnoxious. After all, who do I think I am? How could I for one minute be remotely as wise as my great uncle?!" And soon, a tug of war was birthed in my mind. One minute, I would dream my dream, and the next I would lecture myself about having such silly thoughts. Yet, my dream won the war and grew and grew as the weeks and then months passed. It was during this time, that I first started to notice 'the voice'. I noticed that I had started to hear this familiar wise voice inside my head. I noticed that I would hear this voice whenever I asked myself questions about what to say or what to think about one thing or another. It didn't matter if it was important or trivial. This voice always seemed to have an answer…and always a wise answer.

I also noticed that my friends and even my family would just naturally start coming to me more frequently to solve their dilemmas or to seek out my counsel. This voice in my head would tell me what I should say, and I would say exactly what I was hearing. It soon became widely accepted that I seemed to be growing in wisdom as a kind of gift or talent. Then one day, without any fore warning, our wise old great Uncle Owl came by for another visit. This time around he paid close attention to me and would single me out for long and interesting conversations. At first, I felt really shy and embarrassed, because others continued coming to me for wisdom even though great Uncle Owl was sitting right there! So, almost out of desperation, I very shyly and uncomfortably confessed to great uncle that I was hearing this "voice" of wisdom and discernment in my head. To my surprise, great uncle just nodded and smiled. He looked me right in the eye, held my gaze and said, "I know, son, I know". You can only imagine my astonishment!"

Your turn

Have you searched out your heart?
Have you stumbled across that treasure chest that has your name
all over it?
Is the excitement of your dreams short lived as you let your
present reality sink in?
Do you have a tug-of-war playing in your mind?
"My dream is great! Fantastic! It is achievable"…vs.…. "My
dream silly and impossible, no-can-do"
Are you aware of the things that just come easy to you? Your
gifts, your talents?
Are you aware of things that others come to you for?
Things that you naturally already give to those around you?
Do your gifts and talents line up with your hearts desires?

____

____

____

____

____

____

____

____

____

____

____

40

Chapter Seven

Tawny could feel his own excitement growing as William continued his story. "This look of encouragement from great uncle filled me with delight! You see, up until that moment, I had started to believe that I was going crazy. I thought that once I let my secret out, the secret about this voice in my head, everyone would believe I was totally loopy. They would definitely laugh at me and maybe even push me away as some weirdo. They would no longer seek out my wise counsel. Great Uncle Owl just chuckled at all this and then started to give me a simple yet profound understanding of what was happening."

"You see, he patiently explained to me that I had learned how to hear God's voice. I had known about God and I believed in God, yet I had no idea that this voice was His. This was almost unbelievable! Why would God choose to speak to a little owl like me? Then great uncle taught me that it is actually normal and all creatures are able to hear Him too if they choose. Some creatures are gifted in hearing Him really clearly without much practice or effort. And yet, other creatures learn to hear His voice through spending hours listening for Him. Then he said, "Son, with this gift comes great responsibility. You have been given this dream because this is what God has created you to do. Your calling is to be His voice for the creatures that have not discovered how to hear Him on their own yet. You are to share His wisdom, counsel and love with those who are willing to listen. You must pass on every word that God specifically shares with you for that creature. Exactly as you hear it. Don't add your own comment, don't leave anything out. If you continue to do this, God will trust you and use you greatly. He will send you all over the place on all sorts of assignments. Sometimes these missions will have to do with opening the eyes of creatures that can no longer see their dreams. Sometimes it will be to speak courage into the heart of one about to step onto the path towards living out their dream. Sometimes you will have the hard task of pointing out to someone that their dream has turned cold and icy and desolate. Some missions will be easy, yet others will require you to dig deep in search of His great encouragement and discernment. Yet, even in the difficult missions, you will just know that you know that this is what you were made to do"

"Great Uncle Owl then went on to explain that these missions were what brought him his greatest pleasure and fulfilment. He explained how God gives each and every one of his creatures a dream. He often hides the dream like hidden treasure, and then calls us to search for it. He doesn't force it on us or force us to pick it up. He gives us complete freedom to choose to fulfil our dream or to turn away from it. If we would only stop and rest enough to catch a glimpse of our dreams, to see how marvellous our dreams are, to see the treasure in them. Then if only we would search, and keep searching until we found them. If only we would then hold onto the dream tightly to let it grow and then actually follow our dream, then we would watch in wonder as amazing things would start to happen."

The two birds sat in silence for a while, Tawny was left to ponder all he had been told. How this wise old owl had once been young and many years earlier had been in the same spot that Tawny was now in. He thought about the courage this wise young owl must have had. This wise young owl had dared to follow his dream, to take his call…and now he had lived a great, full, purposeful and happy life.

As Tawny lost himself in his thoughts, William was also left thinking. He was remembering back to the beginning, to those early days. He could only shudder to think how his life could have turned out had he not had the counsel of great Uncle Owl and the courage this gave him to fly and to follow his dream. Just thinking these thoughts grew his resolve that he was not going to let that happen to his little friend Tawny. He was excited about this evening, because he knew that his story had held the answers to many of the questions that Tawny had not yet even considered asking. He knew that what Tawny needed to hear on this night was words of knowledge, encouragement, and most of all, words about identity. These were his favourite conversations. In fact, it was these conversations that the wise old owl knew he was born for. This was what he lived for.

Before the wise owl spoke again, he waited for the familiar voice of his Maker. He knew that this next news would come as a great surprise to Tawny. Maybe even a shock, so he wanted to deliver it gently, wisely, and word for word as he knew he should.

Your turn

*Are you aware that God has given you your own unique dream?
Have you held on to your dreams? Have you shelved them away?
Do you need to search again and dust the cobwebs off of them?
When you have found your dream do you dare to do something
about it, because just maybe this is where you will find your joy,
your fulfilment?
What would you miss out on if you choose not to follow your
dreams?
What if you choose to leave them on the shelf to gather more
dust?*

Chapter Eight

"You see, Tawny, my young friend, you are an eagle—a beautiful, wedge-tailed eagle. You have been created to soar high, high, high in the sky! One of the gifts in your treasure chest of gifts is the gift of astounding vision. Your vision is among the sharpest of all of God's creatures! You were created to see things with astonishing clarity, even from the greatest heights. You can see detail that your young friends are not able to see at all!" Tawny could not believe his ears. His first thought was that he had never for a moment stopped to consider that he could see things that the others couldn't. Thinking back now, it was as though a missing piece of a puzzle had slotted into place. Suddenly it made sense why Lulu seemed to miss almost half of what he saw. They would often end up arguing about the lizard or spider that Tawny saw and Lulu swore was not there! The other lorikeets would often chirp about how Tawny just made things up about what he saw so that he could feel important!

The wise owl continued, "You were created to enjoy savanna grasslands and have an immensely adventurous spirit. This is why you have such a heartfelt longing for these things! Your time has come. You are ready to leave the shade of this giant mango tree that you have come to love and call home. You are ready to soar, to conquer, to be the great bird you were created to be!" Tawny sat back astounded. He was at a total loss for words. His head felt as though it were spinning. Why hadn't he heard this before? Why didn't he know this? Or had he quietly known this all along? He had sensed that he was very different to the lorikeets and the pigeons. Why had no one told him about any of this? Not even Mr Pigeon who said he knew everything important that there was to know! And even Lulu, his best friend! Why did she not mention this to him?

William, reading his thoughts sat quietly and gave Tawny space. He needed space to process his thoughts, to feel all that he was feeling. Then after what seemed like a long time he spoke again softly. He explained to Tawny that no, his family had no idea about the things of eagles. They knew that he was different and loved him for who he was to them. They knew that his presence in the great tree had helped to keep their home safe from snakes and other predators. But beyond knowing he was different, they had no idea. They supposed that Tawny was just there, and possibly had always been just there. "You see, they are totally different creatures to you and even to each other." The old wise owl went on to explain "These others are created to live here in the giant shade of this mango tree. They are living out their dream already. This is why none of them can share your same feelings or your dreams." They would have had other different dreams come to them about other missions or desires, but they definitely had no desire for the things that Tawny dreamed of.

Wow! This was all such a completely new revelation for Tawny. Yet, it also all made so much sense. Of course, this is why Lulu and all her cousins always seemed so happy playing their funny games, scouting out flowers and bees! It is because that is what their dreams are made of!

"Tell me again William" asked Tawny, "Who did you say I am?" Again William told him. "Dear Tawny, you are a beautiful, wedge-tailed eagle. Your kind does not usually live in giant mango trees and they certainly don't know about eating mangos!" he chuckled. "You love to soar and fly and swoop and dive. You are a great bird of prey. That is why you delight in feasting on rabbits so much! None of the other birds in your tree were created to eat meat. That is why you have always been left on your own to enjoy that feast!" Tawny sat quietly for what felt like a long time, taking this all in. When he finally spoke again, William could sense his acknowledgement leading to a growing sense of hurt and frustration. "So how on earth did I get here? How did I get to be living in this silly giant mango tree after all?" he asked angrily. "That is not important right now," answered William softly and wisely. "What is important is what you decide to do with your new knowledge? Now that you know who you are, and what you have been created and designed for, what are you going to do next?"

Tawny pondered the wise old owl's words and realised that he felt far too tired to be angry anyway. In fact, he now realised just how exhausted he was feeling. "I think I need to get some sleep now William. This has been a long evening. Thank you. Do you mind if we talk about this all again in the morning?" William knew that all this new knowledge would take a while to settle in Tawny's mind. Before he said his goodnight, he felt to share one more nugget of wisdom.

"Tawny, there is this great wise proverb that I learned a long time ago. It goes like this:

"It is the glory of God to conceal a matter, but the glory of kings to search out a matter."

You will have many glorious days ahead starting from tomorrow to search out the answers to all the questions buzzing in your mind right now. So go, son, sleep well, and yes, we will continue this conversation as the sun rises in the morning." Tawny flew up to his favourite spot in the giant mango tree to settle in for the night. He made himself comfortable in the familiar twists of his favourite gnarled branch and lay back gazing up at the bright wonderland of stars in the sky. As he settled down, he let his mind travel back over his happy life so far in the comfortable shade of this great tree he had always called his home. He thought back over happy memories with Lulu and all his friends. Within a few minutes he felt like a complete mix up of happy and sad as he struggled to keep his eyes open. "What am I going to do?" he wondered… and soon drifted off into a deep, deep sleep.

Your turn

Do you know who you are? Do you have any idea about what you have been created for?
Have you noticed things that you love doing that others don't?
Do you see things in a way that others just don't?
Are you ready to find and take hold of your purpose and joy?
Are you ready to leave the shade of your comfort zone?
Are you ready to say goodbye to mediocre, to boredom and frustration?

____

____

____

____

____

____

____

____

____

____

____

____

____

Hiding In The Shade

Chapter Nine

Tawny woke up the next morning feeling energised and excited. All night long he had dreamed of swooping, diving and soaring. As he woke further, he remembered that something significant had shifted within him the previous evening. He soon spotted William having a sunrise moment with Mr Pigeon and with steady crystal clarity, the previous nights conversation replayed through his mind. Ah, he sighed, "So. I am an eagle. A beautiful wedge-tailed eagle…hmm". He slowly shifted his gaze down to his feet, then over his belly and then spread his wings out wide to take a good hard look at them. It felt as though he was really only in this moment seeing himself for the very first time. This new fresh knowledge did feel like a treasured gift. He admired his gift and turned it over and over in his mind. As he did so, he felt a great knowing excitement rising in his heart and in his soul. It was in this moment that he realised that his life would never be the same again. This was the day that everything would change. This was the day that Tawny would start to live as an eagle. Then he had another thought, "Hang on a minute! What does life even look like as an eagle? What now? What next?"

Almost as though the wise owl were once again reading his thoughts, he greeted Tawny cheerfully, "Good morning, young Tawny, my eagle friend!! How did you sleep last night?" Tawny smiled and replied "Good thanks… I dreamed… "I know," replied the owl knowingly. They sat for a moment in comfortable silence, focusing on the fresh morning breeze and the morning waking up sounds, now so familiar to Tawny. After a moment, the owl cleared his throat and asked, "Tawny, what will you do now that you know who you are?" Without a moment's hesitation Tawny answered "There is only one thing to do! I am going to fly up, up, up, high in the blue sky and I am going to head south west.

I am going to keep flying until I see the vast savannah grasslands you speak of. There I will search out and meet another eagle just like me. Together we will soar through the skies, doing dives at breakneck speed, and loop-the-loops and when we are exhausted with pleasure, together we will perch on the edge of cliff tops where we can see out for miles and miles. We will take in all the exquisite detail around us and figure the adventure out. I am going to discover all that it takes to be a great wedge-tailed eagle. I am going to discover the pleasures of all the other food there is out there for me. I am going to say goodbye to this tree that I love and have called home for so long. I am going to say goodbye to these creatures that I love and who have loved me back, because now I know that it is actually far greater for me to be out there where God has created me to be and where he has called me to, rather than to stay here in this comfortable shade."

Now, it was Williams turn to look at Tawny in awe! He realised that no matter how often he had seen this before, he would always continue to be amazed at how God's creatures instinctively knew when they were certain that they had tasted their own calling, seen their own unique dream, purpose and mission. It is as though their heart and soul and mind are finally all in agreement and they know they have discovered their unique purpose! William let out a great deep hoot-hoot and Tawny felt an unfamiliar kind of peace settle inside of him. Today was the beginning of the rest of his magnificent life. "What will you say to the others?" asked William? Tawny thought for a moment and then replied, "I will tell them my new truth. I will tell them of the longing in my heart. I will tell them that I love them dearly, and yet I need to say goodbye. I will thank them for being my family, and I will remind them that we will always be family, no matter how far away I am." William could see yet another realisation and a sadness creeping over Tawny's face. He knew this day would not be easy for the little eagle.

Tawny felt a lump growing in his throat. For the last few hours he had been so focused on his new identity and what this meant for him, that he had not given any thought to what this would mean for his beloved home and family. He felt as though his heart, which moments ago had swollen like a balloon filled with new found joy, was now deflating as another reality sank in. "Oh no!" he silently screamed in his mind. "Why did this all have to feel so hard and so complicated!" William watched as Tawny wrestled with his will and his emotions. He knew the 'tug-of-war' in Tawny's mind, so he gently spoke another wise truth to the little eagle. "You know Tawny, you will always remember how to find this great old mango tree and this family you love so dearly, and you will always be able to come back to visit any time you choose." Hearing this felt as though another piece of the puzzle had been slotted in its place. He felt his balloon heart of joy swelling again and felt a surge of happiness like he had never quite felt before.

Your turn

Now that you have identified who you really are, do you see yourself differently?
What things need to change?
What do you need to give yourself permission to do?
What do you need to let go of so that you can go out and walk in your purpose?
What are you afraid of? What are you afraid to lose?
Are you ready to soar and conquer?

Chapter Ten

So William and Tawny gathered the other residents of the great mango tree around for what they explained to be an important family announcement. Lulu and her cousins were immediately sent into a flurry of excitement at the sound of an important announcement, and so the chirping word spread quickly through the tree and surrounds, and before long everyone from the banks of the brown river nearby to the outskirts of the great mango tree was gathered to listen to the wise old owl. William puffed out his chest and spun around his neck to make sure no one was missing and that everyone was listening. For the next few minutes, he shared the reason for his visit.

He re-introduced Tawny to them all as their own beautiful, wedge-tailed eagle! Suddenly, it felt as though time stood still. There was silence. Even the breeze settled and the air felt as though it too was holding its breath. They all cast their eyes on Tawny in awe. It was as though they were all seeing him for the first time. Tawny blushed as he noticed them all scrutinising him from head to toe. He used all the effort he could muster to keep himself from flying up, up, up and away. He turned his focus back to what William was saying in time to hear him say "So, to all of you who are a part of this lovely family here in your giant mango tree, this news does mean that a few things may change, so I now invite Tawny to share with you just what this news has meant for him".

The silence continued as Tawny bravely stepped forward in front of all these familiar creatures he loved. "Hi everyone" he spoke softly. "This news that William has brought to me brings me both great joy and great sadness. Great joy because I now understand why I have long since had dreams and desires that none of you seem to have. I also understand why I am so different to you all. I am different in size, in colour, in what I eat and in what I enjoy. William has explained that the things I long for, deep in my heart and soul are the things that eagles are created for. I long to fully live as the great eagle I know I can be, the great eagle that God has created me to be. Yet today, I am also filled with immense sadness, because I know that in order to live out my life fully and greatly as a wedge-tailed eagle, I need to leave you all. I need to leave this giant old mango tree and all of you who I love so dearly. I need to go where my heart is calling me to go. And even as my heart calls me to go and pursue these other adventures, a piece of my heart will always be here with you."

Tawny paused and looked over at Lulu. He held her gaze and watched as the knowledge of what he had just shared began to sink into her comprehension. A shadow of stunned sadness passed across her face. The chirping that had started up, once again grew completely silent. It seemed as though the creatures had stopped breathing and the slight breeze had decided again to stop breezing. Tawny knew that this was a moment he would remember for as long as he lived. It felt as though something in his heart had cracked, yet he felt complete peace. Then suddenly, as though a spell had been broken, there was a burst of babbling, chirping and mayhem. All the creatures seemed to cry out their protests at once. "Don't be silly Tawny!" "Of course you shouldn't just leave because you are an eagle!" "You belong here! You always have and always will!" "But you are a part of this family!" "We will make you king over our tree if you will just stay? Please!!"

William looked across at Tawny and their eyes met. The two birds shared a deep understanding nod. Suddenly, Tawny swept up into the sky. Up, and up, and up he flew. All the other creatures forgot their protests and turned to watch him. They watched and watched until he had become just a tiny speck in the sky. "Where did he go?" squealed Mrs Pigeon. "Now see what you have done, she reprimanded the others". "Now, now dear" muttered Mr Pigeon in astonishment. This news had been almost too much to bear! They all continued to gaze up into the sky. Some were sure they could still see him, some just couldn't see him anywhere… then suddenly, Lulu pointed and shouted "There! There he is!" They all watched in utter amazement as Tawny nosedived back down to earth at break neck speed. They all held their breath in fright.

At the last moment, Tawny broke his dive and turned sharply to swoop to the left, then up and up again, into a loop-the-loop and a swoop back to the right. The crowd of creatures gathered below soon forgot about all their dismay as they watched the majestic little eagle perform his beautiful eagle dance for them. As he swooped, they sighed. As he loop-the-looped again, they clapped. As he nosedived, they whistled. Tawny finally swooped so low over the crowd that they all ducked and laughed, and then he landed. They rushed towards him, surrounded him and babbled and chirped with excited awe. "Where did you learn to do that? Can you teach us?" William stood back and chuckled at the mayhem. He knew for certain that now Tawny would follow his dream and prayed that he would also learn to follow God's voice.

Your turn

How does it feel when you realise that some things will need to change if you were to even consider your dreams?
What would you need to walk away from so that you can step into your dream?
Is anyone going to try and stop you…only because they love you?
How do you feel when you start to live out your dream for others to see?
How will you respond when those around you try to change your mind about your dream?

Chapter Eleven

The Shade Will Suit Some, but Not Everyone

And so Tawny spent the rest of that day sharing all his many dreams with the others. They hung on to his every word. He sounded so brave, yet none of the other creatures could honestly say that they had any of his same desires. Yes, they wanted to fly as high and would love to learn how to swoop and dive at such break neck speeds, but that was where it ended for them. When Tawny started sharing about travelling to far off places, to the unknown, tales of catching snakes and rabbits and little wallabies, the others definitely did not share these desires! Later that afternoon, Lulu and Tawny flew a little way off to have a quiet break from the others. "I don't want you to go!" chirped Lulu. "I know" whispered Tawny back. "Will I ever see you again?" cried Lulu in despair. "Of course!" chuckled Tawny as he wrapped his wing around her shoulder. "Of course, I will come back. William said that no matter where I am or how far I go, I will somehow always know how to find my way back here to you all. I know he speaks the truth. I know I will always be able to find my way home." Lulu could sense that

Tawny had made his mind up and was seriously leaving. She felt better knowing that she could always hope that he would come back for visits. "Please visit often, Tawny!" she chirped. "I am going to miss you terribly". "I will miss you all too Lulu."

"Please understand that I need to go. This adventure is part of my story. If I don't go, I know I will be miserable and then even you will get tired of hanging out with grumpy old me!" Lulu smiled through her tears. She knew that what Tawny was saying was true. It was at this moment that she understood that something had already shifted and changed. Even if he did stay, things would not go back to how they were before. So bravely agreeing, she gave Tawny the biggest lorikeet hug she could and flew off to hang out with her cousins.

As evening settled in, Tawny felt very sleepy. This had been a huge day. His emotions had felt like they were all over the show. He said his last goodnights and made his way to his resting spot. He felt more than ready to leave the giant mango tree the following morning. As he was collecting his thoughts and getting ready to sleep, William sidled up to him. "Tawny," he said, "tomorrow I will also be on my way. Before you go to sleep tonight, there are just a few final things I feel I need to share with you."

"You know how before I arrived for this visit you had these dreams? You had these stirrings in your heart and you knew things could change and probably needed to change? You felt unfulfilled with things as they were. Well, pay attention to how that felt. Whenever you feel similar stirrings, you know that God is up to something. Tawny, you need to start paying attention to how you hear God's voice. You will soon know the difference between your own voice inside your head and His. This brings me to the next point. Tawny, God has a plan for each and every one of his creatures. This means he has a perfect plan specifically for you! Living out His plans for your life is where you will find your biggest joy and fulfilment. It won't always be easy though. Along the way, there will be obstacles, there will be trials, there will be big decisions to make, and there will be fears."

"Mmmm, fear!" murmured William. "Fear is an important enough reason on its own to learn how to discern God's voice. Some days, you may feel an uneasy sense of fear about impending danger. You fly into an area and suddenly you just know you've got to get out of there! This may be God steering you clear of some danger ahead. To discern this kind of fear and then to fly away from it will be very wise. On other days, however, you may recognise a different kind of fear. You may fear some of the trials you know you need to overcome in order to get to where you long to go. You may fear that you will fail at some things. You may fear not being strong enough, or "eagle" enough. To fly away from these kinds of fears will be foolish. These kinds of fears require prayer, faith and trust in God to get you through. So, how do you know which is which you may ask? … The truth is in your heart. Listen to your heart. When you know that going through the fear will get you to where your heart longs to go, then face up and go through. When the fear is for true danger, your heart will let you know. God's spirit will let you know. When you take all your courage and face up to your fears and push through regardless then, dear Tawny, this is when you get to uncover your most precious God-given treasures."

Tawny understood what the wise owl was saying, and nodded his understanding. "Thank you, William" he replied. "So my little eagle friend," said William, "It is time for me to say goodbye. Until we meet again." The two birds embraced and then settled down to sleep.

Your turn

Have you shared your dreams with others and been told they are crazy?
Does it seem as though no one else sees life the same way you do?
Do you doubt yourself?
Do you know that God has perfect plans for your life?
Do you know that when you walk in His plans, you will find joy and fulfilment even when things are not easy?
Do you know when your fear needs you to face up and push through so that you can meet your purpose?
Do you trust that Gods plans for you are good?

____

____

____

____

____

____

____

____

____

____

____

____

____

Chapter Twelve

It Will Get Hot and Sweaty out in the Sun

When Tawny awoke the next morning, a little before sunrise, the wise old owl was nowhere to be seen. He had left during the night. Tawny too decided it would be easier to leave before the others woke up. He had said his goodbyes the night before and was ready for the first day of the rest of his life to begin. So, off he flew, up, up, up into the clear blue sky. When the giant mango tree no longer looked so huge, but looked rather like a little shrub far down below, he let out his loudest eagle shriek and then, filled with exhilaration and anticipation of the fabulous adventures to come, he turned and headed off in a south westerly direction. He felt more energised and alive than he could ever remember feeling! "I am actually doing this!" he thought. "I am actually finally living my dream!" he shouted out to anyone or anything that could hear him. He let out yet another great eagle shriek. "Today, I will fly and fly until I find those vast savannah grasslands which William told me about," he declared with great resolve.

And so his journey began. He flew and flew for what felt like hours. The sun was now high in the sky and the further south west he flew, the hotter the day became. Eventually, he knew that he had to stop for some rest. So Tawny flew down lower until he spotted a few shady trees near a small trickling river where he could rest, have a drink of water and hunt for some lunch.

Feeling a bit tired, but still more alive than ever before, he landed on the branches of an unfamiliar old tree. He looked around at the all new unfamiliar territory and felt a vague sense of unease drift across his mind. "What do I think I am actually doing?" he thought. He looked out at his surroundings as far as his amazing sharp eagle eyes could see and realised with an inkling of doubt and a sinking feeling that nothing, not-one-single-thing, looked familiar! Everything looked strange and new and different. How could he have not expected this?

How could he have not thought this through? Of course, everything would be unknown! He had just not had any idea how this would feel. How could he have known? Well, he muttered to himself, "I had better get used to this, because this is how it is going to be for a while!" "I am an eagle. A brave eagle. I am born for this" he reminded himself. And so he resolved to shrug off the slight uneasy feeling and made a decision to be brave and bold about flying off towards this new adventure.

Suddenly out of the corner of his eye, something moved and darted across the ground. He quickly forgot all about his vague unease and focussed on the movement he saw. Ah! There! He spotted it—a large grey rat scurrying through some shrubbery a few feet away. We waited and watched until the perfect moment to swoop down on this unsuspecting prey…mmm what a delicious lunch! He tore at the fresh flesh with his sharp beak and ate until there were just a few bones left. He felt full, satisfied and sleepy, so he decided to spend the afternoon exploring the area all the while keeping this new found tree in sight. This is where he would spend his first night away from the familiar giant mango tree and his friends back home.

The next few days were much the same as the first. He spent most of his mornings flying in what he sensed was still a south westerly direction. He would practice swooping, twirling and looping-the-loop during these flights. On one of the mornings, he flew upon a flock of geese flying in a perfect V formation. He flew behind them and watched them for a long while, fascinated that they managed to fly in such precise unison in such a perfect V formation for so long. They flew at such a constant height and speed. He eventually decided to join them, and so fell into formation at the end on one side of the V. Soon his fascination turned to boredom. So he decided to dive out to the right, and swoop back in on them from the left. He would introduce himself and finally have someone to talk to for a while. He definitely did not expect what happened next. The geese were not at all pleased to meet him! And they accused him of messing up their planned flight and formation! They were not interested in finding out who he was or where he was going, and neither were they willing to answer any of the questions he had about whether they knew where the savannah grasslands were or how much further he would need to fly. They just turned him a cold shoulder and told him to get lost and to never ever bother them again.

Your turn

Have you ever started pursuing your dream and it all feels unfamiliar and scary?
Have you started pursuing your dream and then doubt settles in. You ask:"What am I doing?"
Have you started pursuing a dream in excitement, only to feel your excitement nose dive soon into your journey as a new kind of reality sinks in?

____

____

____

____

____

____

____

____

____

____

____

____

____

____

____

____

Chapter Thirteen

When the Sun Starts to Burn

Phew! Tawny had never in his entire life been treated so coldly before. He felt totally rejected, perplexed, and alone. Soon enough, his feelings of rejection turned to anger. What did geese know about eagles anyway! His anger started to feel good. It gave him more than enough energy to fly even further than planned that day. He realised that more than anything on this day he just felt like being angry. He flew faster in his anger. He let his anger run wild. He was angry at his eagle mother whoever she was and wherever she was. Why had she abandoned him? Why did he end up in a silly mango tree where eagles don't usually live?

He was angry at his life and angry at those stupid geese. He swooped and dived in his anger until finally, feeling exhausted, he spotted a tree that looked suitable for the night. So he landed and sat. He sat and looked about and felt that it was all he knew to do in that moment. To just sit. So, he sat and he sat. He stared out over the ground below and let his mind drift.

He was soon so lost in his thoughts that had another eagle flown past just then he wouldn't even have noticed! He replayed the morning's events over and over and eventually dozed off feeling rejected, lonely and hungry. It had been a few days since he had had a decent conversation with anyone. He soon fell into a deeper sleep, a sleep of jumbled dreaming. He dreamt that he flew and flew. He never stopped, but continued flying for days and days, spending each and every evening in a different tree. He dreamt that he was the only eagle on the earth and that the savannah grasslands were just a myth. He dreamt that he could never find his mango tree again. Soon enough this dreaming jolted him awake. He woke feeling panicked startled and scared. What if this dream was really true? What if William had been wrong and didn't know what he was talking about when he told him where eagles normally live. What if William was wrong about everything? What if he would never ever again be able to find his way back to his beloved mango tree and his family?

Suddenly, Tawny was in a frenzied panic! What if this was all a mistake? What if he had made his worst decision ever? His head darted from left to right and back again... where had he just flown in from? Which way was east? Which was west? "Oh no!!" he cried. He felt totally disoriented and confused. He started to sob and sob. All he could do was to sit there and sob. "Oh, if Lulu could see me now!" he mumbled. "I would feel so stupid and embarrassed!" The more he thought about where he was and why he was there, the more he cried. "I am supposed to be an eagle and I don't even know what an eagle is supposed to be like!" he sobbed. As he sat there sobbing, it started to rain. Softly at first, and then more steadily. Tawny loved the rain. He lifted his chin up and closed his eyes. He felt the drops splash gently onto his face and feathers, and then trickle off his body. Before long he started to feel a bit better. The rain felt like it was washing away his tears and his fears. Fears? "Hang on a minute." thought Tawny. "I feel angry. I feel sad. But I also feel fear!" What was it that William had told him on his last night at home about fears? He quietened his mind and tried hard to think back on all the things that the wise old owl had told him. The memory of William's voice came back, floating over him, and he began to remember.

"… Fear … An important enough reason to learn how to discern God's voice. Some days… uneasy sense… impending danger… suddenly, you just know you've got to get out of there! God steering you clear… danger ahead… to fly away will be very wise."

Tawny gasped sharply and held his breath. He glanced around nervously. He listened carefully. He was suddenly on the alert for any movement around him. He looked with sharpened awareness. Nothing. Only the gentle rain. Then he let out his breath slowly… No, he was certain that this was not that kind of fear. This was more a sadness, a doubt. What else had William said? He thought back again until he found the continued thread of that conversation.

"… You may recognise a different kind of fear…

trials you must overcome… where you want to go… fear failure… fear not being strong enough… fear not being "eagle" enough. To fly away from this fear will be foolish… face up to it… require prayer, faith, trust God to get you through… truth is in your heart. Listen to your heart."

So Tawny sat and tried once again to still his breathing and to listen to his heart. He remembered his heart's desire. He remembered believing that the longing in his heart, his dreams of adventure and finding other eagles were all in God's purposes for him. He remembered that if he had stayed behind at the giant mango tree, he would be sort of happy, yet not happy enough, even if the others he loved were still there. He would still be grumpy and longing for this very adventure. He remembered why. Why this adventure was so important. He remembered that this was what he truly longed for and lived for! And that is when he knew that this was the kind of fear he needed to face up to and to push through. Of course, flying into something so completely new and foreign would bring some fear! As soon as he recognised what his feelings were about, it was as though the fear faded a bit. He started to have a strange feeling of peace, even though he still felt lost and alone.

"….God's spirit will let you know … all your courage … face up to your fears and push through regardless … you get to uncover your most precious God given treasures."

Ah, yes, the hunt for the treasure in knowing his purpose. It all made perfect sense. Tawny noticed that the rain had stopped and the air was fresh and crisp. He took notice of his new surroundings with a fresh interest, and realised that not only was he in the most beautiful area he had ever seen, but the sun had started sinking into one of the most beautiful sunsets he could ever remember seeing. Tawny drank it all in with awe. And then he heard it, the still small voice in his head whispering "Tawny, you are courageous and brave. You are my beloved eagle. You were born for this and for all the adventures still to come. I am always with you and will forever always be with you". Tawny quickly looked all around to see who it was that was talking to him. No one. Then he realised that he had just heard God's voice in his spirit. Tawny felt a rush of joy and complete peace flood through him. He just knew that tomorrow would be a good good day!

Your turn

*When pursuing your dreams becomes really hard and requiring
you to dig deep, what will you do?
Will you walk away and go back to how things were before? Or
will you push through?
When doubt sets in, are you able to remember your 'why'? Your
reason to hold on to your dream.
When fear sets in, do you recognise it for what it is?
Do you decide to push through your fear, to face up and keep
going?*

Chapter Fourteen

The Seasons Will Change. It's a Fact

The next day was the mark of a whole week since Tawny had started his adventure. In many ways, it felt like he had been gone from his home for many more days than this. As the sun rose up over the beautiful landscape, Tawny knew that he had made the right choice. He would continue on until he found what he was looking for. He gazed out from his perch in a south westerly direction and noticed some hills not too far off in the distance. He figured he would be able to reach them by midday. So with a renewed feeling of courage and determination, he started his day's journey. He flew for about an hour, and realised that the hills were actually much closer than he had speculated. Before long, he swooped high into the air to get the greatest view of the land on the other side. What he saw took his breath away. There it was! Instinctively, he knew! He had found the great savannah grasslands that William had spoken about. He drifted and slowly circled for a while, just drinking in the incredible view. It only took a few minutes before he had already spotted various delicious choices for lunch. "Oh my goodness" he thought. "This is like nothing I could have ever imagined in my wildest dreams!" "If only Lulu could see all this!" As he was slowly circling, taking it all in, something dark and large suddenly swooped past him from above at breakneck speed and almost knocked him right out of the sky. Tawny let out a shriek as he tumbled towards the earth. He somehow managed to right himself and with rather wobbled flying got his balance back. What had just happened? What on earth was that?

He had just caught his breath and was trying to see what had caused his near crash, when out of nowhere the same big dark thing swooped down again from above. This time, it flew rapidly past with enough distance between them so that Tawny was able to keep his balance and see what this thing was. As it fled past, it let out an amazing shriek. Wait a minute thought Tawny. I've heard that shriek before! I know that sound. He tried to think where he knew it from. Quick Tawny, think. He wondered whether he should follow this big bird and try to catch up to it? Maybe it would be interested in speaking to him. Without thinking any further he instinctively took chase.

"What kind of bird is this?" he thought. One that can fly so fast and swoop so high? "What kind of bird is so big and brown and yet so" ... he struggled for the word... "and yet so strangely beautiful?" He flew on behind the bird, slowly and steadily catching up. Just when he realised he was flying higher than he had ever dreamed to fly before, the bird took a swoop down, first twirling and then diving into a loop-the-loop. Again, without even thinking, Tawny followed suit. As the great bird twirled, he twirled. When it swooped, he swooped. He was now flying at break neck speed, faster than he ever had when the other bird let out another shriek. Suddenly, it dawned on him. That shriek! He recognised it! It sounded just like his own! Only he had never heard that shriek coming from another bird before. Then with wide eyes, the realisation hit him. This was another eagle! He was actually swooping and twirling through the sky with another one of his own. Tawny felt as though he would explode with happiness! This was almost too good to be true! So William had been right after all.

Soon the other bird slowed down and flew low enough to settle onto a branch of one of the savannah trees below. Tawny followed and landed a few feet away. "Finally!" Sighed the other eagle "an eagle who likes to swoop wildly like me!" He introduced himself as Flash. "My family calls me Flash because I love to flash past birds and knock them off balance. Sorry for that mate. I just can't help myself!" he chuckled. Tawny introduced himself, still trying to take the whole experience in. "Where have you come from?" asked Flash. "Why are you all alone?" "How come I have not seen you before?" "Where is your family?" Tawny laughed, "Slow down, Flash! You speak almost as fast as you fly!" So the two birds sat perched together in the little tree as Tawny started to tell Flash his story. Flash listened with amazement. "Wow, mate" he said, "You are the bravest little eagle I have ever met! How cool to have such a great adventure."

"So, let me get this straight," said Flash. "You have no other eagle family?" "That's right" answered Tawny. Flash almost couldn't quite comprehend this. All this talking and thinking had left him feeling ravenous. "Let's hunt for something to eat first, then I will take you to meet the others." "The others?" questioned Tawny. "Of course! My parents and my sister. And then there are also the other creatures that we share our savannah home with. Then if you feel like it, maybe tomorrow you can fly and swoop with me to meet another eagle family who lives nearby." "I would really like that!" replied Tawny.

So, over the next few days, Tawny stayed close to Flash and the two birds flew everywhere together. Flash taught Tawny some new twirling tricks and they both together flew up as high as they could. They laughed and shared stories and soon felt like the best of friends. Flash could not believe all that Tawny shared about the strange mango tree and his strange family that still lived there. He could only try to imagine what these sweet mangos would taste like. "One day when you go back to visit, can I come too?" asked Flash. "Sure", smiled Tawny. "What would Lulu think about Flash?" he wondered. Tawny quickly came to love Flash and his family and they easily seemed to accept him as one of their own. As the days turned into weeks, he was slowly introduced to more and more of their neighbours and eventually it felt like this had truly become his new home.

Your turn

Do you believe that if you push through your challenges and difficulties that your dream will be there waiting for you?
Can you see yourself actually living your dream?
Can you feel it? What do you hear, see, feel, tell yourself?
Will you realise and acknowledge when you are actually living your dream?

Chapter Fifteen

After a few weeks had passed, Tawny started to notice an uneasy familiar feeling creep back in. He recognised it quite soon and knew that it was his familiar old sadness coming back. "What on earth is this coming back for?" he wondered. Surely he should be happy? He had found these amazing savannah grasslands. He had found another eagle family who had virtually adopted him. He had met other eagles too. What was he feeling so sad about? He thought back to William the wise owl and wished that he would magically show up again so that he could ask him these questions. He gave the question of his sadness a long hard thought, and then it dawned on him. "I am sad because even though my life is all so wonderful here, I do miss my home in the giant mango tree along the brown river. I miss Lulu. I miss the mangos. I think I even miss Mr Pigeon!" The more Tawny pondered his sadness, the worse it grew.

"What is wrong with you today, mate?" asked Flash finally. "You are no fun to be with. How about smiling a bit? You look so sad!" Tawny was not sure how to answer. Flash and his family had been so wonderfully good to him. Would it be rude to say how he felt? That he missed the others? The thought of telling Flash why he was so down just felt all wrong. "I don't want to offend or hurt this amazing fun loving eagle and his family by telling them the truth" thought Tawny to himself. He thought about all the fun he had had since meeting Flash. Flash treated him like he was his own brother. So, instead Tawny answered, "I don't know Flash, I guess I just don't feel well today. Maybe that wallaby we ate last night didn't quite agree with me?" Flash was not convinced, but went along with this explanation.

Later that day, as the sun was casting its glorious red streaks into the sunset sky, Tawny told Flash that he just needed to be alone for a while. We would say goodnight now and was sure he would feel better in the morning. So later that evening over their dinner, Flash told his family his concerns about Tawny. He shared with them how down and sad Tawny had seemed that day. Flash's mum smiled and gently shook her head. "Of course, he is sad Flash. I've been waiting for this to happen." "You have?" answered Flash surprised. "What do you mean?"

"Well, I once had a friend a bit like Tawny when I was young like you. This friend arrived at our tree with a similar story. What I mean is that she had also somehow been separated from her own kind as a baby and had grown up I suppose much like our Tawny has. She had seemed happy enough in her first days with us, but quickly became sad. It has taken Tawny a lot longer to feel sad, but I have somehow been expecting it. He feels sad because as much as he has found his own kind and his own place here with us, he has also left another life behind to get here.

As much as this is where he truly belongs, it is natural and normal for him to miss where he came from. When my friend arrived all those years ago she soon became so sad that my father eventually decided to make the trip back with her, back to where she had come from. It was a long trip, but they got there in the end. However, as much as she was happy to see her old friends again, she realised that their lives had changed a bit too. Things were different there. She realised that she herself had also changed by being away and recognised that she would not be happy if my father returned to us without her. So after visiting there for a few days they said their goodbyes and my father brought her back home to us again."

Flash thought about all his mom was sharing. "Imagine feeling sad in your new home and feeling sad because you don't belong in your old home either?" said Flash. Now he too felt sad for what his new friend must be going through. "Who was this eagle, mum?" "How come you have never told me about her before?" "It was so long ago now son, and Ella soon made peace with her move and has loved every minute of being here since." "Ella?" responded Flash in surprise! "You mean our Ella? Who lives across the savannah only a few kilometres away with the other eagle family?" Flash's mum nodded. "And all along I thought she was always just from here!"

His mum continued "So don't worry too much Flash. This is all part of Tawny's journey and the way he is feeling is normal considering his circumstances. Maybe you can take him to visit Ella so that she can share her story with him. Then, if he really wants to, your father and you can make the long trip to fly with him back to his great big mango tree far northwest from here." Flash's face lit up! What a great adventure that would be! He couldn't wait to tell Tawny!

Your turn

Have you felt stuck before? You have moved forward, gone after your dream and then had thoughts about turning around and going back to where you came from, only to find that where you came from has also changed? Time does not stand still.
Do you sometimes miss the simplicity of your mediocre past even though you are aware that going ahead to fulfil your dreams is what will bring you full happiness?
Does the fear of moving forward pull you back towards the safety of your past?

Chapter Sixteen

The next morning, as the first rays of sun tickled the sky, Flash woke Tawny. "Hey, Tawny! You will never guess the story my mum told us last night" Flash almost fell over his words trying to tell the story as quickly as he could. "Slow down Flash!" exclaimed Tawny, trying to keep up with what Flash was saying. He could hardly believe his ears. There was another eagle nearby who would understand! "Can we go and visit her?" asked Tawny. "You bet, mate" grinned Flash. So, the two birds flew over to where Ella and her eagle family lived. Ella greeted them warmly and said that she had been waiting for this visit. Tawny's arrival had reminded her of herself all those years ago. Then for the first time in many years, she spoke freely about the memories of her past. Memories that she had always held close to her heart. She spoke with great fondness of the days before her arrival on the savannah grasslands, yet she spoke with even greater fondness of her life since joining the other eagles.

Tawny hung on to every word she spoke and asked her many questions. Her answers made great sense. It was such a relief for him to be able to speak so freely about how he was feeling and what to do about it. It felt so good to speak to someone else who actually understood what he was feeling! "Should I go back?" he finally asked Ella. "Only you can answer that," she replied wisely. The two birds thanked her for sharing her story and flew back home. Flash knew better than to pester Tawny about going back just yet. He knew his friend had a lot to think over, so they calmly flew home in an uncharacteristic yet comfortable silence.

Tawny spent most of the rest of the day by himself. Flash let him know that he was around and about and if Tawny wanted company, he only had to let out his eagle call and he would join him. So Tawny spent the rest of the day in serious thought. Should he go back? What would he be going back for? What would it give him to go back? What would it give him to stay? What would he lose if he didn't go back? These questions went around and around until he had answered them all. Finally, before the sun went down, he felt like he needed a good half hour to just spread his wings out and to fly. So he let out a loud eagle call for Flash to join him, and together the two young eagles sped off. Up and up and up until they were just two little specks in the sky. Down they swooped and twisted at incredible speed, looping-the-loop, laughing and shrieking. Tawny knew then that he had come to the right decision. Once more he felt at peace and truly happy.

Later that evening, over dinner, Flash asked, "So, Tawny, what have you decided? Are we taking you back north for a visit?" Tawny chewed and swallowed slowly before answering. He looked up at Flash, and then the rest of his family before answering. He knew his answer. He was just not sure how to begin to explain it. As if reading his mind, Flash's dad spoke gently. "Whatever you decide will be absolutely fine with us. We have not sat in the position where you sit now. We can't feel what you must be feeling now. There is no need to explain yourself. We will not judge and we will not question your decision". He looked directly over at Flash as he spoke these words.

Tawny smiled and nodded gratefully. "After a few hours of thinking," he replied, "I have come to a decision that I somehow just know is right for now. I have decided to stay here and not to go back just yet." Flash's face fell. He was so looking forward to the adventure of flying back with Tawny and now that was not going to happen any time soon. "I will convince him later" he told himself. Then Tawny continued, "I may decide after a few months have passed to go back for a quick visit, but for now I know I must stay here with you. That's if it is okay with you all?" "Of course it's okay Tawny!" cried Flash's mum. "You are part of this family now! I hope you know this!" Tawny beamed. "Thank you everyone" he smiled back. He really did feel like he had finally found his home.

As they settled for the night, Flash tried to convince Tawny that he should think again about going back for a visit sooner than later. How could he even contemplate not going back now! They were his other family after all and they would be missing him. Tawny smiled over at Flash. "Flash, I know you would absolutely love the adventure he chuckled. Don't worry, the minute I decide it's time to go you'll be the first to know!" After a bit more thought, he added. "Hey Flash, why don't we plan an adventure of our own, somewhere neither of us has been. A wise owl once told me that as long as we pay good attention, we will always be able to find our way back home. I found you after all, did I not?" Flash could hardly believe that he had not thought of this himself before! Of course! They both had a great desire for adventure and could easily plan something. He would speak to his dad about it in the morning.

Your turn

*Great questions to ask when you are not sure about turning back
or going forward:
What will I gain if I go back? What will I lose if I go back?
What do I gain by going forward? What do I lose going forward?
What other options are also available to me?*

Chapter Seventeen

Over the next few months, Tawny and Flash spent every minute of every day together. They soon began to introduce themselves as brothers. They flew out on many adventures together. At first, Flash's parents agreed to one night only journeys, but as the two eagles became wiser and more experienced, they were allowed to go for longer. They always came back with colourful stories of their courage and bravery. The parent couple listened with delight as they recalled the adventures of their own youth. They recognised that Tawny joining their family was a blessing to Flash. Flash had a tendency to be rather wild, and Tawny seemed to keep him just well enough out of harm's way without dampening his need for adventure. To them it was a win-win for everyone.

During their travels, Tawny and Flash met many other eagles as well as birds and creatures of other kinds. With Flash's energy and spunk, and Tawny's unusual mix of calmness, wisdom and adventure all rolled into one, they made a notable pair. Soon, they were known far and wide and were loved by many. Tawny was amazed at the numbers of creatures he met along the way who carried a familiar cloud of sadness around with them. Their sadness was like a mirror reflecting who he had been before he had set off to find his own treasure. Because he knew those clouds so well, he had the gift of noticing them over others. Flash had no discernment for these sad clouds, but Tawny could see them so clearly. So, whenever he had the chance, he would side up alongside the sad creature and would gently share parts of his story.

Tawny remembered back to his early conversation with William the wise owl. How William had said that he knew what Tawny was feeling before he had even told him. So now he knew how William had known these things about him all those months ago. He chuckled to himself as he realised that he had become much like the wise old owl, only he was a wise young eagle! What Tawny also realised was that the response from each creature to conversations with him was so similar to how he himself had responded to William. He realised that so much sadness was caused because the creatures were living as they thought they should by copying everyone else around them. They were living on 'autopilot' without even recognising that they were sad! They had not stopped to think that perhaps they were different to others around them. Perhaps they had been given a different purpose to those around them. Perhaps they had a different treasure inside, a treasure to be searched for and to be found. A treasure to share with the world.

The one thing that surprised Tawny was that some of these sad creatures were just sad without reason. They had not yet noticed the dream God had sowed into their hearts. It was as though they knew that where they were was not bringing them joy, but they had absolutely no idea what their joy would even look like! It was as though their dreams had come to them totally unnoticed or else they had just been swiped away almost as soon as they had shown themselves. Maybe they had known them once upon a time, but they had hidden them so far away that it was hard to find them again.

The ones who knew their dreams were easier to help. Tawny would share with them that these dreams were in fact a gift from God and most likely their purpose and their calling. This meant that they were definitely worth pursuing. He encouraged them in the knowledge that following their God given dreams and living them out would bring them full joy, peace and happiness. Yet, he also warned them that the journey towards their dreams would require a big dose of bravery, courage, trust and faith. Just because their dream was from God, and was uniquely made as a perfect fit for them, didn't mean that the road would always be smooth and easy. The great news, however, was that if they could be brave and follow their God given dream, God would be there every step of the way to help them through the scary times, the difficult times and the challenges. And most of all, he encouraged them that no matter how tough, it would definitely be worth making the journey.

He shared his own story, right from way back before his dream had even settled on his head that fine day a long time ago. He shared how he had wrestled with it, how he had wanted to throw it away because it brought him such unhappiness. And then, he shared the wise words he had learned from William and the amazing happiness that he would not exchange for anything right now! Many creatures would follow his advice, and he heard many great stories from creatures who did have the courage to follow their dreams. He also saw many sad clouds never leave their creatures. Some creatures were just too comfortable in their sadness below their clouds, and in the shade of their own giant trees to make any changes. Luckily, Tawny had the wisdom to know that that was okay too. He had planted the seed in them, encouraging them to search out the treasure in their hearts. Maybe, just maybe one day they would find the courage to take their journey.

Your turn

If you have uncovered your heart's treasure, and have had courage to pursue it, who can you encourage and inspire to do the same?

Who can you share your story with so that others will be inspired to search out their hearts, to find their own treasure and to make their own journey to let it shine for others?

____

____

____

____

____

____

____

____

____

____

____

____

____

____

____

____

Chapter Eighteen

My journey from frustration, to searching and discovering my own unique treasure and what I am doing with it now

Hello Friend,

I hope you have enjoyed this story. It is no secret that I wrote this book because I have a similar story. I grew up in a beautiful home with a large loving family. I have three brothers and many cousins, aunts and uncles. My parents were both actively involved in our lives and we shared many adventures. My life as a child was enviable. I was greatly blessed. I never wanted for anything (of course, I desired stuff I didn't have… as any kid would…but you get the idea.)

And then I grew up! As a teenager finishing school, I really had no idea what to do with my life as far as a career choice goes. I did know that I wanted to help people somehow and wanted to work with people who were in need of something. So, by chance, I found myself studying medicine. I say by chance because when I am honest about it, I really had no desire to specifically be a doctor. It just ticked the boxes I knew I wanted to tick, and somehow I managed to get the marks I needed to be accepted into the training program.

A few months into my training, I had met with a number of students who were studying the same subjects that I was, but had not been accepted to study medicine specifically. I would listen to their stories of how they had absolutely desired their entire life to study medicine and there was absolutely nothing else they would want to do. They just hoped and prayed to get accepted into the program later down the line. Some never did. Wow! This blew me away. Here I was. Little me. Given this gift of study when others would kill (well almost) to be in my shoes! So, I decided there and then that if this is what I had been given, I had better hang on to it and make the most of it. The thing is, the hospital was my giant mango tree, and even though I was happy enough, so I thought… this was not my real desire. I just had no clue what my desire would even look like if I were given another choice.

So, I did what I knew best. I carried on. It did not come easy for me. It was hard work. I became just so blinded by what I needed to do to keep on passing, to get to the next rotation that I just never noticed the clues. Clues like "Oh, wouldn't it be great to rather be the occupational therapist or the radiographer, or the theatre nurse or the social worker…" I would wonder about wishing I was just about anyone else, just please not the doctor!!! I would think these things daily but would not pay attention because, after all, I was so lucky be in the program and sooner or later I would be the doctor! That is when my pride kicked it. Of course, I was supposed to want to be the doctor!

My family was so proud of me…. and oh the things I could achieve one day. I would listen to my peers banter on about doing this procedure or that one, and I would sit with a knot in my stomach and my brain screaming "Walk away! Find something else! Something you love!!" But how could I walk away? I was now 6 years in, almost qualified. I had 6 years of friendships I somehow thought I would lose if I left… and what would my family think of me? What would my friends think? Besides, if I did walk away, what on earth would I do? So, I stayed in the shade of my tree. Comfortable in being given the next thing to do. The next assignment, the next exam, the next patient. If I just kept doing the next right thing then I would be fine and wouldn't have to think about the mess of having made the wrong decision. After all, how bad could this career be?

Let's fast forward a few years. Now I am married… to the best hubby ever! He is a doctor too. We are both in private practice and we now have two young children. Two beautiful boys. I decide to work only part time because I do want to be home with my boys in the afternoons. I think I am happy.

After all, I have a happy marriage, fabulous kids and incredible friends… it's just this career I silently wish I can ditch! And now I have entered that great war. The war between "stay at home mums" and "working mums". If only my job was not so all consuming I often thought. Before long I felt like a pathetic doctor because I was not available to my patients around the clock (as doctors should be)… and I felt like a mediocre mum because I was always looking at my phone to check that I hadn't missed any patient calls. (I had a whole lot of patients on Insulin therapy who had my number in case of emergency). Then there was the keeping up with all that is new in medicine. This new drug, that big conference, those continued professional development things… And there was always that niggling fear about what if I slipped up or made a mistake!

Then a kind of miracle happened. My husband came home with an offer to train further overseas. We grabbed this opportunity of course, because it was his desire, and subconsciously I felt like I could just have a break. This was my chance to clear my head, to get new perspective… I was being asked to step out from the shade of my tree and into the sun for a moment. I felt really excited by this. Here we were in a new country. Everything was new and exciting for a moment, and the excitement of finding my new way forward was exhilarating!

Once I had settled the boys into new schools and had figured my way around grocery shopping, cycling everywhere and all things new, I started my search. I read books, attended church meetings, joined book clubs and even a cycle club. I made new friends and curiously observed all that was going on around me…all the time searching for clues. Then reality hit. If I could go back and choose all over again, what would I do? I had no idea! None! I felt panicked, I felt stuck. I was not trained for anything else. You see, I still had no concept of life outside of the framework of study and the work I was trained for. I looked at new courses available. What if I picked another wrong one? And so, eventually, out of exasperation and deflated enthusiasm for something new, I decided to go back to medicine! Yeah, I know! Well, I gave it a go.

I had to sit exams again. EEK. I studied hard for eight months, all the while knowing that this was not my desire, yet trying to convince myself that it was. I spent those eight months close to tears with a knot in my stomach, all the while everyone telling me that that was great that I was getting back to it. I nearly drove myself crazy, not to mention my husband. Then one day, it all came to a head. I failed the exam. I was delighted! What a waste of time and energy and money that had been! Yet now, I knew with complete certainty that I had closed that door.

I still went through a process I did not expect. I mourned the loss of a great career. Now I was just a wife and a mum. (HELLO!!!!!) Now in my later years, I realise that many would give their eye teeth for this God given privilege. I have been able to be available to my kids and my husband. I have had the privilege of making the great journey to uncover my treasure and to discover my God given calling, my passion and my love. The first thing I needed to discover was that my career did not define me. It was just a big tree whose shade I tried to hide in. That was huge for me. I discovered that I was significant and had purpose even without a 'career'. I was significant because God had created me and breathed life into me. I am significant because I am completely loved by Him.

My treasure unravelled rather slowly… You see, I was so caught up in wanting to do the right thing and to be the right thing. I did what I thought others expected. If someone said ''jump", I said "how high?" I did go out and work. I studied again so that I could lecture. I lectured in anatomy, physiology and pathology which I loved. I developed training material and trained at a medico-legal company. I did a bit of editing. And I noticed that once again, I had gone back to that tree…. the one where I let my career define me. When would I learn?

Then about 18 months ago, I booked myself into a three-day long life coaching intensive. This was a course where you were trained in personal development tools rather than receiving coaching individually. I know how to be a good student. I am intelligent.

So I went in thinking that I was going to learn a few interesting things and who knows what would come from it? I had no idea what was about to unfold. During those three days I felt like I had found the key to Pandora's box inside of me. I was a mess. I sobbed snotty tears. I cried tears of laughter. I discovered some big nasty limiting beliefs I had somehow let in along my years. I discovered how I had chosen to limit myself, to see life through some warped filters. I was able to see how I was so busy trying to mould myself, to make myself fit into someone else's treasure chest rather than searching out my own.

I remember doing this exercise about our values. I couldn't even define values, let alone tell you what mine were! We were then later asked to give a metaphor for where we saw ourselves at that moment. And there I saw it. I was a baby eagle, in its nest. I had not yet learned to fly, but would soon be kicked out of that nest and would somehow miraculously just know how. I would be able to fly because that's what I was designed to do. I was gifted and talented at that. I didn't have to study for years and years. I was a natural. And there was my clue. I started my new journey into a brand new awareness of myself. The me who God has uniquely created. He has given me gifts and talents and purpose.

His word says that his purpose is to prosper me, not to harm me. To give me hope and a future! Jeremiah 29:11

His word says that we are to delight ourselves in Him and he will give us the desires of our heart. We are to commit to Him, trust in Him and He will act on our behalf. Psalm 37:4,5

His word says that he is a God of peace, not confusion. 1 Corinthians 14:33

His word says that it is He who works in you to will and to work for His good pleasure. Philippians 2:13

His word says to not be conformed to this world, but to renew your mind that by testing, you will be able to discern the will of God, what is good and acceptable and perfect. Romans 12.2

His word says to keep your heart with all vigilance, for from it flow springs of life. Proverbs 4.23

His word says that where your treasure is, there your heart will be also. Proverbs 25:2

I have come to a place where I am able to search out my gifts and talents, and I am also aware of what burdens my heart. Who do I feel the call to help? What do I feel compelled to do that I am good at and that serves Him? That is where I find my purpose, my fulfilment and my joy. I can finally come out of hiding in the shade. I am able to step into the sun where His full light shines through me and where I can continue to search out the treasure He has put in me, to bring Him glory and to live the life I was created to live!

Thank you for taking this journey with me.

Love

Kathryn

Notes

Do you see yourself in Tawny? Is his story also your story? The questions through this book are self reflective to help shine a light for you to see where you are in your own journey. This may leave you with a greater sense of awareness of the life you are not living, but would like to. If you find yourself hiding in the shade and wanting to take that first step out into the sun, I would like to invite you to join me in an on-line self paced program especially created to follow on this book.

Visit me at www.fufilled-life.com to find out more

I have been fascinated by people I meet along my journey who seem to know what they are here for and are successfully walking in their calling. I have included some interviews with these ladies which I know will encourage and inspire you too.

Interview with Jessica Nazarali

Jess Nazarali is a Business Strategist & Certified Master Coach for women who want to build thriving coaching businesses and become the 'It Girl' in their industry. This is what she had to say during our interview on the subject of discovering your purpose and following your dreams.

Me: I am curious to discover how people like yourself seem to 'have it all together' as far as living out your purpose in life. You have a good assurance of what your purpose is and you are an inspiration in how you walk out your purpose with boldness, clarity and certainty. This is encouraging for those on the outside looking in who do not have this same assuredness about their own purpose.

Jess: Thank you, I appreciate you saying that.

Me: Have you ever been in a season where you felt you had no idea of your purpose in life?

Jess: Yes, definitely. In April 2011 I had just returned from a holiday in the US and Canada when my boyfriend proposed. At that time there were a lot of family and friends around, and everyone was so excited for me. I returned to Australia and was telling my best friend that I was engaged. I remember how she was also so excited for me. She was looking at me and my ring and started planning my wedding in her head there and then! Yet for some reason I was feeling so sad and so down. I began wondering what was wrong with me. I should be happy! I had just gotten engaged! What I realised was that even though I was marrying someone I really loved, and had a roof over my head and quite a good job, I was feeling sad was because I wasn't living out my purpose.

I remember thinking "Oh my gosh, living life this way for another 30 or 40 years will just be soul destroying!"

So I was newly engaged and should have been feeling really happy, yet I remember feeling sad and confused and quite angry with the world. I had studied hard at university and had good grades and I really thought that this would lead to me having a career that I loved. A career that would enable me to climb the corporate ladder. Yet I discovered pretty quickly that that wasn't going to be the case. So, yes, I definitely can relate to not being clear in my life purpose.

Me: Thanks Jess, so what I am hearing you say is that during that season of your life, even though you were purposefully getting married to the person you loved, there was something else not in alignment with what you knew you were purposed for?

Jess: Yes, definitely. The reason I felt so frustrated was because I knew I could "do better" with my life. I knew I had more to give. I told myself "You are better than this!" I felt I had so much more to contribute than I was currently giving. I realised that in a lot of ways in my current job I was playing it safe. I was just going to work, just going through the motions, not really living. In many ways I felt disappointed in myself. I told myself, "This is the kind of life you have created for yourself."

Me: So you had a great awareness at this time that how you were living was not how you wanted the next 30 or 40 years to be. However, were you aware of how you did want your life to look rather than how it was then.

Jess: No, not massively. I remember when I was 11 somebody asked me what I wanted to do when I grew up. I remember thinking that I wanted to either be a ballerina, or to work in personal development. I always knew I wanted to help people. I just didn't exactly know how. So when I was newly engaged and yet sad, no, I didn't know how I wanted my life to be. I remember from April to September 2011 I went through a period where I wasn't particularly joyous about anything in life, so I started researching a lot. I would google things like "How to start a business", "How to start a blog", "How to find your life purpose", "How to find your passion". I also started to read a lot of personal development books at the same time. So I definitely started looking, but I wasn't yet clear on what I wanted my life to look like.

Me: To have the awareness that you are not happy and then to proactively spend the time researching what you could rather be doing is incredibly proactive. So how did you begin to navigate your way forward to stepping into something else that was more in alignment with what you felt was your purpose at that time?

Jess: I knew I was really unhappy and I also knew that I would not be happy working in the same job for the rest of my life, so I was really dedicated to working out what else I could do. I guess what really started to change things for me what that I started reading blogs. I read many health, wellness and personal development blogs. I had been reading these blogs for about two to three months when I started getting this voice in my head that said "Jess, you should start a blog".

Yet I thought mmm, I am not a writer. I studied business at university. I had a lot of friends who had studied communication and journalism who were really good writers, so I said "No. Blogging is for good writers, so why would I write a blog?" "Who would read it?" Yet this voice in my head kept on getting louder and louder.

So I started a blog and then found a program online that taught how to write, set up and grow a blog. This program cost $500 which at the time this felt like a whole lot of money to spend on something online. At that stage I had never even bought an ebook before. The program was all online with no group calls, so I wondered if it was a scam… this whole online thing. Yet, what kept me thinking about the program was that I didn't know much about what I was doing and didn't feel good about my blog. I kept wondering who would read my blog. So I closed my laptop and went away. I said to myself out loud "If i am meant to take this course, I need a sign". I was really in angst. Was this the right thing to do or not the right thing to do? The next morning I was scrolling through my emails and came across an email about the program that said "50% off. Limited time only". This was my sign! I felt I was meant to take the program. So I signed up to the course and paid $250.

Then fast forward 18 months later: I now have a blog. It's getting pretty good traffic. I have sponsored posts. I have advertisers. I have PR agencies sending me things to blog about. I realised that by having this creative outlet I soon became a lot happier in my job. I felt like I had a passion and purpose outside of work where I felt I was giving back in a small way. I had a message I was sharing with the world. What most human beings want is to know that they are of value and can contribute in some way. This is what the blog gave me when I was starting out.

Me: So what you are saying is that even though you were still in a job you didn't really enjoy, you had another area of your life that you felt was more what you were created for. Do you think that it is okay to have areas in your life that are not in line with what you feel your purpose is, so long as you have other areas that do align with your purpose?

Jess: Yes, definitely. I have seen this with many of my clients as well. They are a lot happier in their job when they have an area of their life that does fulfil them. I think it is like a relationship. You could put all the pressure on that one person to be everything to you, yet if you have other friends also, who have other interests, it takes the pressure off that one person. I have seen many people say "Oh, this job isn't really that bad after all".

Me: Have you noticed your life purpose change as seasons in your life change?

Jess: Yes, definitely. From starting out with my blog, I eventually moved into blog coaching. This wasn't really in my plan, but people started asking for my help. So I discovered coaching and realised that I really enjoyed this. As I mentioned earlier, I knew I wanted to help people and to be a teacher. Coaching allowed me to do that. So, yes, my purpose has changed and I have grown and transitioned and I am sure my life purpose will continue to change.

Me: It is like you are on a journey. So as you continue this journey and you grow, things unfold and your purposes grow and change. What is the most helpful tool you have to discover the next step in this journey of walking out your life purpose? What do you do to keep on this journey and to not end up back where you were in April 2011?

Jess: I measure my success and how I am doing based on how happy I am for the most part. A really good marker is to ask myself: 'How happy am I feeling at the moment? How in alignment do I feel about the work that I am doing?' If work is really hard or a struggle, it may be because I need to hire different people or to put different systems in place. There have also been times when I have thought "I don't feel I am lit up by this project even though it is going smoothly." So I decide on something different. So for me it's taking time to check in before I take on a new project or change direction. I try to really think things through before I make a big commitment.

Me: What I am understanding you say is that sometimes you move quickly and then realise the project is BIG or hard…yet if it still lights something up, you go ahead regardless of the difficulties. If you step into something and it feels flat then maybe it is not a direction to go into.

Jess: Yes, so I'll give you an example. Let's say I was releasing a program and there were a lot of issues throughout the process, yet I was excited about working with the women in the program and the concept of the program. I would keep going and sort through the challenges because I am really in alignment with the end goal. On the other hand, if there are many issues and I feel I am not actually interested in the topic any more, then I would look to changing direction.

Me: Have you had a situation in your journey where you are doing work that does not interest you yet others around you still encourage you to move forward in that area because it is what they want you to do?

Jess: Yes, I have a recent example. I was talking to someone successful in the industry who gave me advice that I nearly took on. However, I realised that this advice did not apply to me. I realised that I had a choice to not take on what she was advising. Even though she has done really well and has had a lot of success, what she was saying was not true for me. So I think it is really important to have your own vision and to stay true to it. Others can give opinions whether or not you want to take them on

Me: If you meet someone who feels lost about what they are meant to be doing with their life and you could give them one piece of advice, what would it be?

Jess: I think a lot of the time people do know what they are meant to be doing or they do know the first step to take, yet they are afraid to take action. For example, I knew I wanted to help people or to teach, I just didn't know what form that would take. So, it's just that. Go with what you know for sure. It can be "How do I help people?" "What would interest me?" Then go and explore that. Give yourself permission to further explore what you feel you want to do.

Me: What if someone says, "No, I really don't have a clue?" What do you say then?

Jess: I would refer them to a coach who helps specifically with this. However, I think a lot of the time people don't actually give themselves enough time to sit with themselves. They may have a family and commitments which make life really busy. They take 10 mins before going to bed and think, "I can't believe this is happening to my life", "This isn't what I am meant to be doing and I don't know what is". Sometimes what we need is a whole week off. Leave where you live. Go on vacation somewhere either by yourself or with someone who is supportive. Then give yourself the space to explore. I think this is a big part of it. When you are out of the daily grind, things do come up. Are you going to ignore it or are you going to follow it up even though it is scary?

Interview with Emma Mullings

Emma is a radio announcer, TV presenter and recording artist. She currently hosts the mornings show on Sydney's HOPE 103.2FM 9am – 1pm weekdays. This year she released two new singles: "Skinny Roads" and "Dream Again".

Me: Have you ever been in a season where you felt you had no idea what your purpose in life was?

Em: I think the two most important days in a persons life is the day they are born, and the day they discover why. For me, meeting my creator at 22 years old put me on the path to discover that 'why'. I can only speak out of my personal experience, and for me, my relationship with God has been my guiding factor to discover my 'why' and my purpose. It is a beautiful thing to actually be able to ask the person who knit you together in your mothers womb, with a plan and purpose for your life in mind - "What on earth am I here for?" and He actually does answer.

Me: Have you ever had a season in your life when

you've been aware that the things taking up most of your time were not well aligned with what you knew you were purposed for?

Em: Yes! Sometimes these things aren't even bad things. There are many good things that can fill up our time and sometimes even good things can be a little off centre to the 'God' thing we were purposed to do. I think it's a good idea to come aside from all the noise for a little inventory at times. I know that is hard to do, I have kids and a full time gig and no extended family around to support! I totally get that it's hard. Even if it is a few nights in a row where you turn your phone off and focus on the end goal and purpose, put pen to paper, and really take the time to reassess your time and if you are spending it the best way possible. Working back from the end goal always has helped me. (everyone will go through a season as long as we realise it is a season and not a life sentence).

Me: Do you feel (or have you previously felt) that in some areas of your life you are fulfilled in walking in your purpose, yet in other areas not so much?

Em: Absolutely! One thing I have really learnt in this is the difference between a season and a life sentence. It might be a season that I am in, in an area of my life and it doesn't mean it's going to be forever. If I am faithful and diligent with the small that I have in my hand, God will trust me with the big. I think of it like cooking a good recipe - if we throw all the ingredients in at once it will make a big mess, there is a reason and a method and adding other things later in the mix often gets the better end result.

Me: Have you noticed your life purpose change as the seasons of your life have changed?

Em: For me my purpose is really to help people and specifically help them heal. My life story is one of restoration and healing and I am acutely aware that my healing is not just for me, it is for others too. This outworks itself in so many different ways. In some seasons the facet it outworks itself in is more media based, the field in which I work, through interviews and shows. In other seasons it is more church based, where I serve a lot of my time, in other seasons it is more music based, through the songs I write. In the season of being a new mum it might be just buying another mum at the park a coffee and being her listening ear for an hour. Whatever season I am in, the end purpose is the same - to help people heal from things that have kept them inhibited so they can walk free and be all they were created to be. (spiritual, emotional, mental, relational)

Me: What is the most helpful tool you have used to discover and step into your life's purposes?

Em: For me it is definitely finding a relationship with God. He is the one who made us and He is the one who had that original plan for our lives. He knows the details of what we have been through and walked through, and he cares about the details. He is full of answers and wants us to fulfill the purpose we were created for more than we do!

Me: You meet someone who feels lost about what they are meant to be doing with their life. What one treasured piece of advice would you share with them?

Em: I often ask people three things,

"What did you want to be when you were 5 years old?"

Often this is a key and clue to what they were created to do. That childlike dream they had for their life before distractions of finances and day to day stresses took over.

"What would you do if money was not an issue?"

If we didn't HAVE to work to earn $$ for our rent or mortgage each week, what is it that we would do with our time.

And the last question I ask them is

"What is it that irritates them, that gets them mad!?"

This is often a key to their purpose. For example, injustice is something that has always rubbed me the wrong way - more than the average! And it is because of that, that I've been able to really help 'war brides' in Uganda through different charities. What made me mad also motivated me to do something about it and make a difference in someone else's life. We were all created to solve a problem and we are all a "10" at something, and often that thing that makes us mad might be a problem we were created to solve. We can't do everything but we can all do something.

Notes

Notes

135

Notes